LATINOS IN BASEBALL

Alex Rodriguez

Jim Gallagher

Mitchell Lane Publishers, Inc.
P.O. Box 200
Childs, MD 21916-0200

LATINOS IN BASEBALL

Tino Martinez	Bobby Bonilla	Roberto Alomar	Pedro Martinez
Moises Alou	Sammy Sosa	Ivan Rodriguez	Bernie Williams
Ramon Martinez	**Alex Rodriguez**	Vinny Castilla	Manny Ramirez

First Printing

Library of Congress Cataloging-in-Publication Data

Gallagher, Jim, 1969-
    Alex Rodriguez / Jim Gallagher.
       p. cm. — (Latinos in baseball)
    Includes index.
    Summary: A biography of the Seattle Mariners' power-hitting shortstop, Alex Rodriguez.
    ISBN 1-58415-010-6 (lib. bndg.)
    1. Rodriguez, Alex, 1975- —Juvenile literature. 2. Baseball players—United States—Biography—Juvenile literature. [1. Rodriguez, Alex, 1975- . 2. Baseball players. 3. Dominican Americans—Biography.] I. Title. II. Series.
GV865.R62 G34 2000
796.357'092—dc21
[B]   99-059366

About the Author: Jim Gallagher is a former newspaper editor and publisher. A graduate of LaSalle University, he lives near Philadelphia. His books include *The Composite Guide to Wrestling* (Chelsea House) *Pedro Martinez* (Mitchell Lane) and *The Johnstown Flood* (Chelsea House).
Photo Credits: cover: ©Ben Van Houten/Seattle Mariners; p. 4 Jacobsohn/Allsport; p. 7 Ben Van Houten/Seattle Mariners; p. 24 Jim Commentucci/Allsport; pp. 29, 31 Ben Van Houten/Seattle Mariners; p. 39 Jason Wice/Allsport; pp. 40, 41, 42, 45, 51, 53, 54, 55, 58 Ben Van Houten/Seattle Mariners.
Acknowledgments: This story has been thoroughly researched and checked for accuracy. To the best of our knowledge, it represents a true story. This story is neither authorized nor endorsed by Alex Rodriguez or any of his representatives.
Dedication: To my brother Dan, the best guitar player I know.

TABLE OF CONTENTS

Alex Rodriguez, Seattle's All-Star shortstop, is one of the best young players in baseball today.

CHAPTER ONE
The Best Young Shortstop

Seattle Mariners' star shortstop Alex Rodriguez stepped to the plate and stared at pitcher Jack McDowell. There was one out in the first inning of the September 19, 1998, game against the Anaheim Angels. Rodriguez, the second batter, waited patiently as McDowell's first pitch sailed by the outside corner of the plate. Then he fouled off the next offering to even the count at 1 and 1.

McDowell's next two pitches were out of the strike zone, and Rodriguez knew that the next pitch would probably be a good one. The Anaheim ace wound up and fired a fastball toward the plate. Rodriguez swung, connecting with the ball and sending it arcing high into the air. For the 40th time in the 1998 season, the ball landed in the stands—a home run.

As Rodriguez stepped on home plate after circulating the bases, he accepted backslaps and high fives from his teammates. Alex Rodriguez was now the newest member of the select 40-40 club. Only two other players in baseball history had ever hit 40 home runs and stolen 40 bases in a season. Jose Canseco was the first to accomplish the feat, in 1988, and Barry Bonds did it in 1996.

But more importantly for Alex, the homer gave the Mariners a 1-0 lead. Although the young star is one of the league's best hitters, he has always put the team's success ahead of his own personal goals.

Ever since he became a full-time player, Alex Rodriguez has made hitting a baseball seem easy. In his first full season, 1996, he led the league in hitting with a .358 average—the highest batting average ever by a rookie, and the best average in the American League by a right-handed batter in 67 years. That season he was among the league leaders with 36 home runs, 123 runs batted in (RBIs), 141 runs scored, and 54 doubles. In 1997 he accomplished another rare batting feat in a June game against the Detroit Tigers when he "hit for the cycle," getting a single, a double, a triple, and a home run in one game. And in 1998 he hit more home runs—42—than any other shortstop in history, then matched that figure the next season.

Rodriguez is considered the best of an outstanding group of young shortstops, including 1996 Rookie of the Year Derek Jeter of the Yankees, Boston's 1997 Rookie of the Year Nomar Garciaparra, Alex Gonzalez of the Toronto Blue Jays, and the Mets' Rey Ordonez. When *Sports Illustrated* polled the general managers of the 14 teams in the American League, asking them which player they would most like to have if they were starting an expansion team, Rodriguez got the most votes. "Someday he might bat .400 and hit 60 home runs," said Red Sox general manager Dan Duquette. "He's the best young talent I've seen in years." Former Seattle batting coach Lee Elia, who had managed in the majors, told *Sports Illustrated*, "I had Mike Schmidt in Philly, Don Mattingly in New York, Ryne Sandberg in Chicago, but I haven't seen too many guys who can get their bat through the hitting zone any faster than

Alex. With his ability, there's no telling what he can accomplish."

Cleveland Indians general manager John Hart agreed. He compared the young shortstop to one of Alex's childhood heroes, Baltimore's Cal Ripken Jr. A 6-foot-4, 200-pound power hitter, Ripken redefined the shortstop position when he came onto the major-league scene in 1982. Up to that point, shortstops often were good fielders but poor hitters. Baltimore's previous shortstop, Mark Belanger, is an example typical of the period: he was one of the league's best fielders at the position in the late 1960s and 1970s, but he managed a career batting average of just .228 with 20 lifetime homers. Despite his lack of offensive skills at the plate, Belanger played for 18 seasons.

By contrast, Ripken combined Gold Glove fielding with excellent hitting, accumulating more than 3,000 hits and 400 home runs. He won Ameri-

Alex hustles after a shallow popup. While he's best known for his hitting, Alex also takes pride in his fielding skills, and is one of the league's best, defensively.

can League Most Valuable Player Awards in 1983 (.318 average, 27 home runs, 102 RBIs) and 1991 (.323, 34, 114), and set a major-league record that may never be broken by appearing in 2,632 consecutive games.

Rodriguez—nicknamed A-Rod by his teammates—is obviously prepared to take over as the best shortstop in the league with Ripken nearing retirement. Most people believe that it's only a matter of time before the 6-foot-3 Rodriguez also wins an MVP award or two. His first season was the best ever by a shortstop, and he finished second in the MVP balloting to Juan Gonzalez of the Texas Rangers. He has hit for a good average—and increased his power totals—every season since then. "[Alex is] a big, physical shortstop like Ripken, but he's a better athlete," said Hart. "He probably has more power than Cal, and he might be a better all-around hitter."

"I just want to get better. I love it when people say that [1996] was a career year for me, that I can't do it again," Rodriguez tells reporters when asked about his future. "I love to hear people say that. That's a challenge to me, a major challenge."

CHAPTER TWO
A Baseball Childhood

Victor and Lourdes Navarro Rodriguez already had two children, Joe and Susy, by the summer of 1975. On July 27, the family grew by one more when Lourdes gave birth to a second son. The couple gave their youngest child a big name, Alexander Emmanuel, though they usually just called him Alex.

The Rodriguez family lived in New York City. Victor and Lourdes had moved there from the Dominican Republic, a small nation in the Caribbean Ocean off the southern coast of the United States. It is difficult to make a living in this poor country, so many people leave to find a better life in the United States. Since coming to America, Victor and Lourdes had prospered. Alex's father owned a successful shoe store in Manhattan, and his mother worked the night shift at a local automotive plant.

Some of Alex's earliest memories are of his father, who watched him during the day while minding the store. It was Victor Rodriguez, a former baseball player in the Dominican, who first gave Alex a bat and ball when he was about two years old. "[He was] so good to me, actually spoiled me because I was the baby of the family," Alex later recalled.

While the young Alex loved New York, his parents were eager to leave the Big Apple and return to the Dominican Republic. By the time Alex was four, Victor and Lourdes had saved enough money to retire and return to their homeland. They purchased a four-bedroom house in Santo Domingo, the capital of the Dominican Republic, and headed south with their three children.

Alex soon learned that the people of his new country were crazy about baseball. It was—and still is—the most popular sport on the island. Over the years a number of talented baseball players have come from the Dominican Republic, including pitcher Juan Marichal, who compiled a Hall of Fame career in the 1950s and '60s. Two superstars from the Dominican Republic who are just a few years older than Alex are Chicago Cubs slugger Sammy Sosa and hard-throwing right-hander Pedro Martinez of the Boston Red Sox.

Under the eye of his father, who had once caught for a Dominican pro team, Alex began to learn the finer points of the game. "I always wanted to be like my dad," Alex later admitted.

The four years that Alex spent in the Dominican Republic—surrounded by aunts, uncles, grandparents, and cousins—were great. Unfortunately, the good times wouldn't last. Victor and Lourdes lost a lot of their money on bad investments. They were forced to sell their dream home and move back to the United States.

Eight-year-old Alex liked his new home in southern Florida. The Rodriguez family had moved to a suburban town outside Miami called Kendall. Alex made new friends, although going to school in Kendall was a big adjustment. Alex spoke Spanish—the most common language used in the Dominican Republic—much better than he spoke English.

But sports was a common ground for the kids of Kendall. Alex started going to the ballpark to watch a local baseball team practice. One day the coach invited him to join the game. Even though he was younger than many of the other players, Alex was able to hold his own.

Afterward, the coach, whose name was Juan Diego Arteaga, drove Alex home. Coach Arteaga's son, J.D., was close to Alex's age. They lived just two blocks away. Soon J.D. and Alex were the best of friends.

However, things were far from perfect for the Rodriguez family. When Alex was nine years old, his father told him and his siblings that he needed to leave their home in Kendall to work in New York. He promised that he would return soon, but he never did.

When Victor Rodriguez deserted his family, everyone was hurt. But Joe and Suzy were older; they had both graduated from high school already. The loss of Victor was hardest on his youngest son, who was just in fifth grade.

"I thought he was coming back," Alex said years later. "I thought he had gone to the store or something. But he never came back. . . . It still hurts.

"From talking with Mom, I found out that Miami wasn't fast-paced enough for Dad, that he wanted to go back to New York and Mom didn't," he added. "They talked but couldn't agree. So he split."

Suddenly, Lourdes was on her own with three children to support. She took a job as a secretary in a

Miami immigration office during the day and waited on tables at a nearby restaurant in the evenings. When she would come home from her waitressing job, Lourdes would let her youngest son count her tip money in order to learn math skills.

There is little doubt that Alex received his penchant for hard work—as well as his understanding of the value of education—from his mother. "All the love I had for [my father,] I just gave to my mother," Alex commented. "She deserved it. . . . She's one of my best friends."

But even though Lourdes made sure that her youngest son never neglected school, his first love was baseball. Alex was amazed at the difference in the conditions between his suburban home in the United States and those of the poor country where he had really started playing. "In the Dominican Republic, playing ball was tougher," he said. "No one had anything. In the U.S., there were $200 gloves and the fields were like paradise."

Alex practiced every day, learning the skills that he hoped would allow him to play in the major leagues one day. "He was very focused from the time he was a child, and wasn't interested in anything else," his mother recalled. In addition, he began to follow the careers of some great major-league baseball players. He liked Detroit Tigers shortstop Alan Trammell and Atlanta Braves slugger Dale Murphy, but a young player with the Baltimore Orioles was his favorite: Cal Ripken Jr., who had made his mark on the major-league scene as a rookie in 1982 with 28 home runs and 93 RBIs.

In addition to being great players on the field, Trammell, Murphy, and Ripken were role models off the diamond as well—a fact that Lourdes Rodriguez always appreciated. "My mom always said, 'I don't care if you turn out to be a terrible ballplayer, I just want you to be a good person,'" Rodriguez told *Sports Illustrated* in 1996. "That's the most important thing to me. Like Cal or Dale Murphy, I want people to look at me and say, 'He's a good person.'"

Joe Rodriguez played baseball constantly with his younger brother. "He pitched to me in our games, and he'd always let me win—until the end of the game," Alex remembered. "Then he'd go on and beat me. It made me want to get better. I'd cry when I'd lose. Then I'd cry when we stopped playing."

Alex was so much better than the other ballplayers his age that he was often invited to play in games with his brother and older boys. Testing his skills against more developed players would prove to be a blessing, helping him to develop faster, but it could be frustrating at times as well. "I was mad about it, because I could never dominate," Alex said.

Alex was also mad and frustrated about the loss of his father. "After a while, I lied to myself," he admits today. "I tried to tell myself that it didn't matter, that I didn't care. But times I was alone, I often cried."

Fortunately, his best friend's dad became almost like a father to the hurting youth. Juan Arteaga brought Alex along when he took his own son to baseball games; he bought them both athletic equipment; and he watched them practice and play games. "He was the father I didn't have," Alex said. "Everything he gave to his son, he gave to me."

Coach Arteaga had a sense that Alex might be good enough to play professional baseball. "One day, my dad told me Alex was the best player he'd ever seen," J.D. Arteaga later commented. "[Alex] was 11 years old. I thought, 'Crazy man, how can you say that?' But now look. I guess my dad was a pretty good scout."

Juan Arteaga introduced both Alex and J.D. to an organization called the Boys and Girls Clubs of Miami, which ran the best baseball league in the city. There, Alex met a coach named Eddy Rodriguez. Eddy had once played minor-league baseball, and he told Alex about some of the star players he had coached with the Boys and Girls Clubs of Miami: Jose Canseco, Rafael Palmeiro, Danny Tartabull, and Alex Fernandez.

Eddy's team sometimes practiced twice a day. The team was so good when Alex was there that they won two national championships and three city championships. Alex even won the league batting title one year.

In addition to playing baseball, Alex loved to watch the sport. He examined players' habits, both at the plate and in the field. "When I got to the big leagues, no one had to tell me that Cal Ripken was a pull hitter or what Darryl Strawberry did with two strikes," he later told Sports Illustrated. "My knowledge shortened the learning curve for me, big time."

CHAPTER THREE
High School Star

During the summer of 1988, as Alex was about to enter eighth grade and a new school, he considered quitting baseball.

In the previous school year, Alex had attended Kendall Academy, where he made the varsity baseball team. This was quite an accomplishment: he was just in seventh grade while most of the other players were juniors and seniors in high school.

But by the end of the school year, Alex was feeling burned out on baseball. "I thought about focusing on basketball instead," he commented in his book *Hit a Grand Slam*. "Mom called a family meeting, and we talked about my options. She convinced me to 'give baseball one more season.'"

Alex attended Christopher Columbus Catholic High School in ninth grade, where he played on the varsity basketball team as well as on the baseball team. However, he was the backup shortstop at Christopher Columbus, and the coach told him that he probably wouldn't get a chance to play full-time until his senior year.

After ninth grade, in 1990, Alex decided to transfer to another high school, Westminster Christian. His friend J.D. Arteaga was attending that high school, and Juan Arteaga urged Alex to enroll there as well. The private school was a well-known baseball power: 29 of coach Rich Hofman's former players had gone on to play in the major leagues.

However, Westminister Christian had an expensive annual tuition of $5,000—more than the Rodriguez family could afford. Alex applied for financial aid to help with the cost, and his mother made other sacrifices so that he could attend the school.

At Westminster Christian, Alex played football, basketball, and baseball. He became quarterback of the football team, wearing number 13 like one of his sports heroes, Miami Dolphins quarterback Dan Marino. Alex also made the varsity basketball team as a sophomore, although he dropped the sport after that year to concentrate on baseball.

His 10th-grade season on the diamond had both good and bad elements. On one hand, he earned the starting spot at shortstop, quite an accomplishment for a sophomore, and the team had finished with a very good 26-6 record. However, Alex was disappointed with his performance at the plate: he managed just a .256 batting average.

Alex's sophomore year was tinged by another, more serious, tragedy than a poor batting average. In the fall of 1990, Juan Arteaga collapsed during a football game. He was flown by medical helicopter to the nearest hospital, but it was too late. To Alex, the pain felt as if he had lost a father again.

"I don't know why Mr. Arteaga died then," Alex said in *Hit a Grand Slam*. "I do believe God has a plan and things happen for a reason. Sometimes we just can't understand it.

"J.D. and I grew closer, as brothers. We shared each other's loss, although we really didn't talk about it much. We gave each other strength."

After his first baseball season at Westminster Christian, Alex started to build up his physical strength. He could bench-press about 100 pounds when he first started working out in the weight room. By the next baseball season, he could bench over 300.

His hard work paid off. In football, Alex had a great year, leading Westminster Christian to a 9-1 record. He was an All-State selection at quarterback. The baseball season was even better. Westminster finished with a 32-2 record and won both the state baseball title and the national high school championship. It was the first time that the Westminster baseball squad had ever been ranked number one in the country. Alex hit .477 with six home runs, 42 stolen bases, and 52 runs scored, and he was selected as a high-school All-American. But he wasn't just a good athlete; Alex was also a good student and made the honor roll.

In the summer of 1992, Alex was chosen for the U.S. junior national team and played with the squad in Mexico. In the fall, he again was an All-State football selection, although the team's season was not quite as good.

Everyone was looking forward to the baseball season to see if Westminister Christian could repeat as national champions. Alex and J.D. Arteaga made college decisions over the winter. Both signed letters of intent to attend the University of Miami on baseball scholarships. With that distraction out of the way, they could concentrate on their senior seasons.

It would be a pressure-filled season. After his great junior year, Alex was considered one of the best baseball prospects in the country. Dozens of baseball scouts showed up to watch every game. So many scouts called for Alex every night that his sister came home from college to help answer the phone. Despite this pressure, Alex came through. He batted .505 with nine home runs and 36 RBIs in 33 games. He also stole 35 bases without being caught once.

Westminster Christian did not repeat as state or national champions. The team was eliminated in a state playoff game—Alex made two costly errors—and finished with a 28-5 record. However, Alex was named the USA Baseball Junior Player of the Year. He also was a finalist for the Golden Spikes Award, given to the top amateur player in the country. This was quite an accomplishment for a high-school student; the award typically goes to a college player. The 17-year-old also won the Gatorade National Student-Athlete Award.

Alex finished his high-school career with a .419 average (124 hits in 296 at-bats), 17 homers, 70 RBIs, and 90 stolen bases in 100 games. He had done nothing to hurt his status as the best high-school player in the country. He was a sure bet to be picked early in the annual amateur baseball draft conducted by Major League Baseball.

Soon, Alex began hearing rumors that the Seattle Mariners wanted to select him with the first pick in the 1993 draft. He was worried. Seattle had entered the American League as an expansion team in 1977 and had a long history of losing. In fact, the Mariners had just one winning season in their history, an 83-79 mark in 1991, and the team had returned to its losing ways the next year, finishing last with a 64-98 record.

Winning was important to Alex, and he wanted to be drafted by a competitive team. But because the Mariners had often finished near the bottom of the standings, they had been able to select early in the amateur drafts. Some of the players chosen by Seattle in the 1980s were starting to make their way to the major-league team by 1992. The best-known was Ken Griffey Jr., the son of a former major-league baseball player, who had emerged in 1989 as one of the game's rising stars. But the team fielded by Seattle in 1993 also featured such future stars as Jay Buhner, Edgar Martinez, Randy Johnson, and Tino Martinez.

The night before the 1993 baseball draft, Alex Rodriguez received a call from Roger Jongewaard, the Mariners' vice president of scouting and player development. Jongewaard told the young infielder that Seattle would probably pick him first in the draft.

On June 3, 1993, J.D. Arteaga held a party, and Alex's friends and family gathered to celebrate while waiting for the results of the draft. Early in the afternoon, a call came: the Seattle Mariners had made Alex the first player selected in the major-league draft.

CHAPTER FOUR
Working Toward the Majors

To negotiate his first professional contract, Alex Rodriguez hired a well-known sports agent named Scott Boras. In the meantime, he joined the U.S. Junior National Team and participated in a pre-Olympic baseball tournament in San Antonio in July. He rapped out four hits in two games, but his season was ended when he was hit in the face with a wild pitch. The errant throw broke his cheekbone; he had to undergo surgery, which ended his baseball season.

Although Alex wasn't playing, other players were taking notice of him. On Alex's 18th birthday, Oakland A's slugger Jose Canseco gave him a German shepherd puppy. Alex named his new best friend Ripper, after his hero Orioles shortstop Cal Ripken Jr.

Alex also struck up a friendship with the ballplayer who had been the first pick in the 1992 draft. Like him, the young man was a shortstop prospect. He was working his way through the Yankees' farm system. The talented player's name was Derek Jeter, and he was playing with a team in the Florida State League. Alex visited him between games and asked him all kinds of questions about the draft and professional baseball.

"[Jeter] had won the USA player of the year honors and so had I," Alex later explained. "More important to me, Derek won the Gatorade Award, for the top student-athlete, and that's what drew the connection for me. He's smarter than me, though. He got 1200 on his SATs. I got 910. My reading comprehension held me back, because we speak only Spanish at home."

The two ballplayers soon struck up a friendship and agreed to stay in touch as each found his niche in the major leagues.

Unfortunately, Boras's negotiations with the Mariners were not going well. At one point, the agent prohibited face-to-face or telephone conversations between team representatives and Alex. Correspondence could take place only by fax. As the discussions drew into late August, Rodriguez prepared to begin college classes at the University of Miami. If he attended a college class before the Mariners signed him to a contract, the team would lose its rights to him and he would be returned to the player pool for the 1994 draft.

At practically the final moment, on August 30, 1993, Rodriguez agreed to a three-year, $1.3 million contract with the Mariners. Playing baseball professionally was what he had wanted to do since he was a child, and now that dream was coming true. "I wanted to be in the big leagues as soon as possible," he said of his decision to sign with the Mariners rather than attend college.

In early September, the Mariners brought him to Seattle and gave him a tour of the city. The team's 23-year-old superstar Ken Griffey Jr. showed Rodriguez around and invited him for dinner. The two hit it off right away and spent the night playing video games. Griffey, a high-school player selected first in the

1987 draft, understood the pressure to perform that Alex was feeling, and he encouraged the younger player.

In the fall of 1993, Alex began his professional baseball career in the Arizona Instructional League. The instructional league is a place where young players can develop their skills to prepare for the major leagues without the pressure of big-league attention. After the instructional-league season, Alex worked out in Miami, spending up to five hours a day lifting weights, running, and fielding grounders.

In March 1994, Alex went to spring training with the Mariners. No one expected a 17-year-old who had graduated from high school less than a year earlier to make the team. Seattle's management sent him to the Mariners' Class-A farm team, the Appleton Foxes in the Midwest League.

To reach the major leagues, young players typically must work their way through several minor-league levels: Class A, Class AA, and Class AAA. Each time a player moves to a new level, he finds the competition is better. A player may be able to get away with making some mistakes at the lowest levels; however, by the time he reaches Triple-A, any flaws in his game—such as an inability to hit the curveball or a lack of control when pitching—will keep that player from ever reaching the majors.

Sometimes the journey through the minor leagues can take four or more seasons. When they sent Rodriguez to Appleton, the Mariners just hoped that their young prospect would develop into a player good enough to play in the majors someday.

Rodriguez proved that he was far too talented to stay in Class-A ball for long. In 65 games at Appleton, he hit .319 with 14 home runs and 55 RBIs. During one 16-game stretch in April and May, he hit .406 with 11 homers, driving in 31 runs. He was selected to play in the Midwest League's All-Star Game, but by the time the game was held at the midpoint of the season, the Mariners had already promoted him to the next minor-league level, Class AA Jacksonville in the Southern League.

In his first at-bat with Jacksonville, Rodriguez homered; he hit .288 with 8 RBIs in his 17 games with the club. After just three weeks, Rodriguez was promoted again—this time, all the way to the major leagues.

It can be dangerous for a young player to be called up to the big leagues so quickly. Sometimes when young players are brought up too fast, they are overwhelmed by the pressure. If they are sent back to the minors, it may be years before they are ready to return to the big leagues again. And at age 18, with less than a year of pro baseball under his belt, Alex was especially young. Very few 18-year-olds have ever played in the major leagues, and only one, Robin Yount, really thrived. (Yount, who was elected to the Baseball Hall of Fame in 1999, came up in 1974 as an 18-year-old shortstop with the Milwaukee Brewers.)

But the Mariners had fallen 12 games under .500, and in the words of manager Lou Pinella, the team "needed a spark." Even though Seattle's best player, Ken Griffey Jr., was leading the majors in home runs after setting a record with 22 round-trippers in the first two months of the season, Seattle had lost 15 of 20 games at one point. "We have a problem here," Pinella said. "If we didn't have a problem, [Alex] wouldn't be here yet."

The manager thought so highly of his 18-year-old prospect that he asked shortstop Felix Fermin, one

For many young players, facing the pitchers at the professional level is a big adjustment. Alex, however, didn't seem to have any problem getting hits off minor-league hurlers in his first full season.

of the team's batting leaders with a .333 average, to play second base to make room for Alex.

"There's always a concern when you start them this young, but we feel this kid can handle it," Pinella told the *Miami Herald*. "He has an abundance of skills, and he doesn't lack confidence. You get vibes from young players. The kid who is scared sits on the end of the bench during spring training. This spring, when I was ready to make my substitutions, Alex always became highly visible. He would grab a glove or bat and stand right near me. He was telling me he was ready, in his own way."

Alex himself admitted to friends and family that he was nervous before he joined the Mariners. He told friends that the team was "crazy" for bringing him up so quickly, and he asked his sister Arlene to pray for him and to "call everyone we know and have them pray for me, too."

His mother drove him to the airport early in the morning before Alex was to make his debut with the team. "Mom, I don't believe it. Is it real? It's a dream, right? Can I do it?" he asked.

"I know you are strong," his mother answered reassuringly. "You aren't trying to be a baseball player. You were born to be one. You will be fine."

On Friday, July 8, 1994, less than a month before his 19th birthday, Alex played his first game in a Mariners uniform, against the Boston Red Sox in historic Fenway Park. His proud mother watched from the stands.

"It was incredible," Lourdes Navarro said after the game. "I kept asking myself, 'Am I dreaming?'"

Alex didn't get any hits, but he did handle all his chances in the field flawlessly. The next day, he got his first two hits as a major-leaguer. "Last year, I would have paid anything to go watch a major-league game," he excitedly told *Sports Illustrated.* "This year, I'm playing in one."

Pinella placed Alex at a locker next to Ken Griffey Jr. He hoped that the veteran star would help the young shortstop adjust to the pressures of the American League.

Alex Rodriguez fielded well during his stint with the Mariners, but he struggled at the plate, hitting just .204 in 17 games. In August, Seattle's management decided to send him down to the Mariners' Class-AAA farm team, the Calgary Cannons, where he could work on his hitting. Although Alex was disappointed, it turned out to be a good move for him. On August 12, the major-league baseball players went on strike, ending the season prematurely. If Alex had still been with the Mariners, he would have had to join the walkout and his season would have been over; instead, he gained valuable playing time with the Cannons. In 32 games against Pacific Coast League pitching, Rodriguez regained his timing at the plate. He hit .311 with 6 home runs and 21 RBIs.

It was an incredible first year in pro baseball for Rodriguez. He had dominated at all minor-league levels and proved that he had the ability to play in the majors.

In the off-season, Alex confidently returned to the place he had originally learned how to play baseball, the Dominican Republic. He was going to have another chance to face major-league pitchers in Winter League baseball. The season was humbling; he batted just .179.

"It was the toughest experience of my life," Rodriguez told *Sports Illustrated* in 1996. "I just got my tail kicked and learned how hard this game can be. It was brutal, but I recommend it to every young player."

CHAPTER FIVE
Playing For a Winner

As spring training began for the 1995 season, Alex hoped he would become the Mariners' everyday shortstop. After all, he had been successful at the Triple-A level the previous season.

But manager Lou Pinella felt that Alex needed more time in the minors. He assigned the 19-year-old shortstop to start the season with the Tacoma Rainiers, a new Class-AAA affiliate of the Mariners.

Tacoma, Washington, where the Rainiers played, was just 31 miles from Seattle. It would not be long before Alex would be driving back to join the major-league club. On May 6, just a month after the 1995 season started, he was called up by the Mariners.

While he was with the team, the rookie was the focus of jokes and pranks by his veteran teammates. "The Mariners have a special rookie tradition for the team's first series in Kansas City," Alex later wrote. "When I got out of the shower after the last game, all my clothes were gone. Instead, I had to sign 30 autographs while wearing a silver dress and balancing in high-heeled shoes. If that weren't bad enough, I had to wear them on the flight home and listen to all the teasing jokes. I laughed along with them."

However, Alex was not laughing when he was sent back to Tacoma a few weeks later. The Mariners

then called him back up to the big leagues. After another short stay, Alex went back to the Rainiers. In all,
Seattle would call him up and send him down three
times. It was very frustrating for the young player.

"Each demotion chipped away at me," he said.
"The last time, in mid-August, I sat at my Seattle locker
with my head down, in tears. I felt drained, defeated."

At one point he even considered quitting pro

baseball and going back
to Miami, where he
could attend the univer-
sity and rejoin his friend
J.D. Arteaga, who was
pitching for the Hurri-
canes. It was his mother
who convinced Alex to
keep playing hard.

Alex did just
that. In his 54 games at
Tacoma, he racked up a
.360 batting average, 15
homers, and 45 RBIs.
At last, on August 31,
he was brought up to
the Mariners for the
rest of the 1995 season,
and he got to be part of
an incredible pennant
race.

The Seattle fran-
chise had never made it

Although Alex was frustrated at shuttling between the Mariners and Triple-A Tacoma in 1995, he was excited to be a part of Seattle's playoff team.

to the postseason since joining the American League in 1976. Even though Mariners pitcher Randy Johnson was having a spectacular season (he would win the AL's Cy Young Award at the end of the year) and designated hitter Edgar Martinez was leading the league in batting, the team was far back in the race for the AL West title. Seattle's best player, Ken Griffey Jr., had been injured and missed most of the season; by the time he returned on August 24, Seattle was 11 1/2 games behind the California Angels for the AL West lead.

But his first night back, Griffey hit a game-winning home run. That sparked the Mariners. During one stretch while Alex was with the team, Seattle won 16 games and lost just three, overtaking the Angels for the division lead.

For the most part, Alex played a minor role as the backup to veteran shortstop Luis Sojo. But he could learn by watching in the major leagues, and he appreciated the chance to be part of a winning team. "It was an awesome experience," he told *Sports Illustrated*. "I was 20 years old. It would have been ludicrous for me to think I should have been in there. I understood my role—I was there to pinch run or fill in if someone got hurt—and it didn't bother me at all."

"I think he learned a lot just being around down the stretch," manager Pinella commented. "Even though we all knew he was our shortstop of the future, it wouldn't have been fair to the guys on the field or to Alex [to put him in the starting lineup]. Our veterans were doing a great job, and we were winning games."

Alex finished the 1995 season with a .232 batting average, five home runs, four stolen bases, 19 RBIs, and 15 runs scored. He batted 142 times in the 48 games he played during his multiple stints with the Mariners.

At the end of the season, Seattle and California had identical 78-66 records. A one-game playoff would determine who would win the division and advance to the playoffs. Seattle, true to its team motto "Refuse to Lose," pounded out a 9-1 win.

The Mariners were excited to make the playoffs, but they knew their first postseason opponent would be tough. Year in and year out, the New York Yankees have been one of baseball's best clubs. The Yankees had won a strong division, the American League East, and were heavily favored to win the best-of-five series over the upstart Mariners. In fact, the Yankees won the first two games, which were held in New York.

As the team's backup shortstop in 1995, Alex worked on both his fielding and his hitting. Here, he goes for a ball in the hole.

31

But the tide turned when Seattle returned to the Kingdome. The Mariners took the next two games from the Yankees to even the series. A final game, to be played in Seattle, would determine which team would advance to the American League Championship Series and which team would go home.

The fifth game was a back-and-forth affair, just as the entire Yankees-Mariners series had been. An eighth-inning Ken Griffey home run—his fifth of the series, tying a playoff record—put Seattle ahead 4-3, but the Yankees tied the game in the ninth, forcing extra innings. The Yankees then scored to take a 5-4 lead in the top of the 11th.

Seattle was three outs away from playoff elimination, unless they could score. Second baseman Joey Cora opened the inning with a bunt and reached base safely. The next batter, Griffey, singled; Cora stopped at third base. Edgar Martinez, the American League's batting champion in 1995, was the next up. In the on-deck circle was Alex Rodriguez.

Martinez ripped a line drive down the left-field line. Cora scored easily to tie the game, and Mariners third-base coach Sam Perlozzo thought he would hold Griffey at third. But Griffey never broke stride, racing home for the game-winning run. Rodriguez, standing to the side of home plate, signaled for Griffey to slide. Tears of excitement welled up in Alex's eyes, and he was the first player to jump into Griffey's arms as the Mariners and their fans began a mad celebration.

Alex later said that winning the playoff series was his most exciting moment in professional sports.

Even though the Mariners did not make it to the World Series in 1995—they lost the best-of-seven American League Championship Series to the Cleveland Indians, four games to two—the team had proved that it was for real. Even more important, the Mariners' play-off heroics had probably saved major-league baseball in Seattle. Over the years the team had had difficulty drawing fans to games, because the Mariners usually lost. Because of the lack of interest, at the start of the 1995 season the team's owners had been considering moving the Mariners to another city. However, people came out by the tens of thousands to support the Mariners when they started winning. That made the owners willing to stay in Seattle, and even to build a new stadium where the team could play.

CHAPTER SIX
Breakthrough Season

Alex spent much of the off-season watching videos. Specifically, he watched tapes of his teammate Edgar Martinez, who had led the American League in hitting in 1995 with a .358 average. "The tapes were three hours long, all his hits from '94 and '95," Alex said. "I watched them about three times a week. . . . If you have a great hitter, if you have a great player, why not take the opportunities to look at them and do some of the great things they do?"

He also worked with Seattle hitting coach Lee Elia, who suggested that the young shortstop shorten his swing. "He came down one day and said he wasn't feeling comfortable," Elia recalled. "We worked four, five days shortening up on it, making him understand that he had enough leverage and enough bat speed through the hitting area that he didn't have to stay long."

When Tony Gwynn, a seven-time National League batting champion for the San Diego Padres, saw Alex Rodriguez in the batting cage during spring training 1996, he knew the young Seattle shortstop was going to have a big year. "Andy Ashby was pitching, the bases were loaded, there were two out," Gwynn said. "Ash is trying to run a sinker down and in on him. He's trying to keep his hands inside the ball and he keeps fouling it off and fouling it off and fouling it off.

Finally, he got . . . his hands inside the ball, inside-outed it right up the middle. I said, he's been working with somebody . . . he's going to have a good year this year."

Gwynn had no way of knowing that 1996 would be Alex's breakout season, that he would put up numbers no other shortstop in the history of the game had ever managed. And it certainly didn't seem that would happen from Alex's first few games. He struggled at the plate, managing just two hits in his first 19 at-bats.

But Alex started to heat up on April 8 with a base hit. The next day he hit his first home run of the season—a 440-yard blast to dead center in Detroit's Tiger Stadium. Over the next two weeks he hit a torrid .375.

A pulled hamstring on April 21 in a game against Toronto forced Alex to the disabled list until May 7; in his first game back, he went 0 for 3. However, he would soon get back into his groove at the plate. On May 12 he had his first two-homer game, against Kansas City, and just five days later he hit his second grand slam of the season. By June 25 he had pounded 15 home runs, including a 450-yard shot that bounced off the restaurant atop Toronto's SkyDome.

From June 19 to July 6, Alex hit in 16 of 17 games. One of these hits, in the final game of this hot streak, was his team record–tying third grand slam of the season. At the end of this run, he had pulled his average up to .341, good for sixth in the league, and had driven in 57 runs in 63 games—impressive numbers for someone who wouldn't even turn 21 for another three weeks.

His emergence as one of the league's best players led, inevitably, to comparisons with Ken Griffey Jr. The Mariners' star had started the season slowly, although by June he seemed to be back to his usual form. Alex handled the situation respectfully. "To me, Junior is so special and so unique, I hate to hear any kind of comparisons," he said. "It's an insult to him. He's the best." Griffey, meanwhile, had good things to say about his emerging star teammate. "He works hard, he's a smart kid, I think he's in the right situation," he told *Sports Illustrated*. "He just has to listen and learn the game. Everyone knows he's going to be a special player."

His performance both at the plate and in the field led to Alex's selection to the 1996 American League All-Star team. He was the youngest shortstop ever to play in an All-Star Game and the 15th youngest player overall. It was an exciting day, even though he was hitless in his only plate appearance.

After the All-Star break, Alex continued tearing the cover off the ball. The Mariners were again making a run at the American League West title and were leading the league in runs scored. On July 18, Alex went 4 for 4; that improved his average to .352, second in the league. On July 27, Alex turned 21; he celebrated by pounding his 22nd home run of the season. That same day, the Mariners locked him up for the next four years, signing their star shortstop to a contract extension worth $10.6 million.

July was a great month: Alex batted .383 and scored in 23 of the 28 games he played. But his August would be even better. Alex had smashed the Mariners' old record for home runs by a shortstop (16, by Todd Cruz in 1982) in July; he hit his 25th homer on August 7 against the Cleveland Indians. His 30th and 31st homers both came on August 21 off Baltimore's Scott Erickson. And from August 16 through September 4, Alex hit in 20 straight games. His batting average during that span was an incredible .457 and included a 5-for-5 day on August 29. He was named Player of the Month, only the sixth time a Mariner had received that honor.

Alex powered his way to the American League batting title by hitting in 52 of his last 60 games to finish with a .358 average. He was the first shortstop to win the American League's batting crown in more than 50 years (the previous winner was Cleveland's Lou Boudreau in 1944). Alex's average was the highest by a right-handed batter in 57 years (since Joe DiMaggio hit .381 in 1939), and he was the third-youngest AL batting champion ever (behind Al Kaline and Ty Cobb). Alex had 215 hits, more than any other shortstop in history. In 65 games, he collected two or more hits.

Alex also displayed unusual power for a shortstop, belting 36 homers and a league-leading 54 doubles. He led the league in total bases (379), and his slugging percentage (.631) was fourth best in the league. His 141 runs scored led the league and set a new standard for shortstops. He was eighth in RBIs with 123.

Defensively, he played very well at the toughest position in the field, committing just 15 errors—five fewer than Cleveland shortstop Omar Vizquel, the league's Gold Glove winner at the position. In all respects, Alex was an important part of the Mariner's 85 wins, the highest total in team history to that point. However, he was disappointed that Seattle finished in second place in the AL West, 4 1/2 games behind Texas, and missed the postseason.

Both the *Sporting News* and the Associated Press named Alex Player of the Year, but in a narrow vote the baseball writers picked Texas slugger Juan Gonzalez for the AL's Most Valuable Player award. In the closest vote in 36 years, Alex finished second, just three votes behind Gonzalez, who had hit .314 with 47 homers and 144 RBIs in 134 games. Some people believed that Alex had hurt his own cause in a late-season interview, when he told reporters that Ken Griffey should be the MVP.

"If I can lose the MVP every year because of my humility, I will lose it every year," Alex later said, although he admitted that he had been disappointed that the two Seattle sportswriters who voted on the award had listed him third and fourth on their ballots and had listed Griffey ahead of him.

"I play this game mostly for the respect of the people in the clubhouse, and that includes the beat writers," he explained. "When not even one of them thought you were the MVP of the team, that hurts me. I would say 99 percent of the players I saw this off-season told me I deserved it. I'm not taking anything away from Juan, because he had a great year."

Alex's year was great both on and off the field. He had become a fan favorite because of his personality.

Unlike some players, he was always willing to meet fans and sign autographs. And after signing his contract extension, Alex had developed an educational program called Grand Slam for Kids. He used the program to encourage elementary-school students to focus on reading, math, physical fitness, and good citizenship. He visited Seattle-area grade schools and talked with the students there. "It's really an honor for me to come here today and spend some time with you," he would tell captivated audiences, encouraging the students with comments like, "It's important to read as much as you can" or "Math is very important, to keep up with Ken Griffey's batting average."

In 1996, Alex Rodriguez put up offensive numbers that no shortstop had ever matched.

Alex talked with reporter Murray Chass about why he makes such an effort to connect with young people. "We have a big responsibility as young men of this game," he explained during the off-season. "We're very fortunate. We have to communicate with the fans, who we really need to get this game back to where it needs to be. It's not just about hitting home runs and making great plays and winning championships. It's getting the fans to realize this is the best game in the world."

Back at home in Florida, Alex returned to the Hank Kline Boys and Girls Club of Miami to see his friend and former coach Eddy Rodriguez. He donated $25,000 to build a new baseball field behind the club

Alex has become a fan favorite because he always has time for others. Here, he lets a young fan try on his batting helmet, then signs autographs (p. 41) for another supporter.

buildings. "No other player has ever come back to this place and given like Alex has," the coach said. "Alex just did it. 'Whatever you need,' he said."

In addition to spending some of the millions from his contract extension on the ballfield, Alex also purchased a house. Although he could have afforded a mansion, the home he did buy was moderately sized: a four-bedroom ranch house in a gated development in Kendall, just a few blocks away from his mother's house. He spent some time painting and decorating his new home over the winter. He also played golf, which had become one of his favorite hobbies, with his friend Derek Jeter. Jeter had won the American League's Rookie of the Year award in 1996 (Alex was not eligible

because of the number of games he had played in 1994 and 1995), and the two spent a lot of time talking baseball during the off-season.

"We talk about how important baseball is to us," Rodriguez said. "We especially talk defense because that's what a shortstop's game should be about. We agree we'd rather go hitless and make some good plays to help the team win than go 4-for-4 and lose. Nothing justifies an error."

"I think we bring out the best in one another," Jeter told *Seattle Times* sportswriter Bob Finnigan. "I'm one of Alex's biggest fans. I talk about Alex around here, my own teammates tell me to shut up."

Alex greets a crowd of his fans after a game. Young admirers can follow his accomplishments—and read his thoughts about the season—at his home page, www.arod.com.

Being baseball's newest and brightest star brought new demands on Alex's time. He traveled to Japan to play on an exhibition all-star team. One of his teammates was Cal Ripken Jr., and the two later visited each other's homes, competed in basketball—Cal beat Alex in a game of one-on-one—and discussed baseball, with Ripken offering tips on playing the position they shared.

During the season, Alex had signed a contract with the Nike shoe company to endorse its athletic products and in the off-season visited Jamaica for a party thrown by Nike for its celebrity pitchmen. He also appeared at numerous charity events and promotions and recorded a commercial for the United Way.

By the time spring training began in March 1997, Alex was exhausted from all the attention. "This is the first time, the first place, I've felt at peace in months," he told the *Seattle Times.* "We must have turned down 80 to 85 percent of the requests, and I was constantly on the move."

But Alex could not relax for long at spring training. After his incredible 1996 season, the pressure was on him to perform. Could he live up to everyone's expectations in 1997?

CHAPTER SEVEN
Back to the Playoffs

Alex started off the 1997 season the way he had left off the previous year. He batted .333 in April—including a 4-for-5 day against the Boston Red Sox April 6. Beginning June 1, Alex got a hit in 16 straight games. He batted .343 during the streak and .358 overall during the month.

But Alex's most memorable day during that hitting streak was June 5, when he managed a rare batting feat. He batted for the cycle, meaning that he hit a single, a double, a triple, and a home run all in the same game. It came in a contest against the Detroit Tigers. Alex was the second batter up in the first inning; he powered a pitch from Felipe Lira out of Tiger Stadium to give the Mariners a 1-0 lead. It was his ninth home run of the year. His next time up, in the fourth inning, Alex hit a single, and he tripled in the eighth inning.

The Mariners had control of the game at this point, with a 10-3 lead, and they scored four more runs in the eighth. This meant that Alex would bat again in the last inning.

Swinging at an outside pitch, Alex drove a fly down the right-field line. As he rounded first, Seattle's first-base coach, Sam Mejais, shouted at him, "Go, go, go!" Alex reached second standing up, beating the throw from right field, to become just the second player in the history of the Seattle Mariners to hit for the cycle.

He was congratulated by his teammates, especially Jay Buhner, who had been the first Mariner to accomplish the hitting feat.

But Alex and his teammates were not the only ones excited about the accomplishment. There had been a special promotion for this game: a fan's name was drawn for each Seattle hitter, and if one of the Mariners hit for the cycle, that fan would win $1 million. A woman from Cashmere, Washington, named Pamela Altazan received the prize. "I can't wait to get home and get my cut," Alex joked afterward.

In 1997, Alex showed that his previous season had been no fluke. He was voted to the All-Star Game again, and finished with a .300 average, 23 homers, and 84 RBIs.

A few days later, Alex was hurt because of his aggressiveness. Racing home in a game against Toronto, he collided with starting pitcher Roger Clemens and suffered a chest injury. He was placed on the disabled list and missed the next 14 games. But when Alex came back on June 27, he showed that the time off had not affected his batting eye by hitting a home run off Anaheim's Chuck Finley in his first at-bat.

But Seattle's attention was not focused entirely on Alex that year, as it seemed to have been in 1996. His teammate Edgar Martinez was among the league leaders in batting, and pitcher Randy Johnson was having an incredible year. Coming back from the injuries that had ended his 1996 season after just five weeks, Johnson's first four victories tied an AL record (16 consecutive wins, dating back to 1995). He set a league record for a lefthanded pitcher with 19 strikeouts in a game against Oakland, and he would finish with 20 victories, a paltry 2.28 earned run average, and 291 strikeouts. With their ace back in top form, the Mariners expected to compete for the division crown again.

But most of the attention was directed at Ken Griffey Jr., who was hitting home runs at a near-record pace. In 1994 Griffey had been on track to break the all-time record for home runs in a season, 61, which had been set by Roger Maris in 1961. However, the baseball strike had ended his chances that year. Now, in 1997, he had hit 30 home runs by the All-Star break to challenge Maris's record again. His run at Maris's 36-year-old mark overshadowed Alex's performance.

But the young shortstop didn't mind. He was especially pleased to be voted the starting shortstop in baseball's All-Star Game. He was the first shortstop in 14 years other than Cal Ripken Jr. to start for the American League. (Ripken started this game at third base.) Alex singled off star Atlanta pitcher Greg Maddux and finished the game 1-for-3.

Alex started the second half of the season well. He collected four hits in a game against Texas on July

10, the third time he had done that in 1997. He had an 11-game hitting streak in late August and got six hits in his final 12 at-bats of the year.

Alex's final statistics for the season were not as good as they had been in 1996. He batted .300, an excellent mark but 58 points lower than his average the previous year. His totals of doubles (40), home runs (23), runs (100), and RBIs (84) were also down, although all were more than respectable figures. But the statistics were not as important to Alex as the fact that Seattle had finished 90-72, winning the AL West by six games over the Anaheim Angels.

It had taken a team effort for the Mariners to win their second division title in three years. Ken Griffey Jr. had fallen short of Maris's record, but his 56 home runs and 147 RBIs were team records, and he would go on to be named the league's MVP. Edgar Martinez had batted .330, one of the best averages in the league. And behind Johnson (20-4), the Mariners had two other strong lefthanded starters, Jamie Moyer (17-5) and Jeff Fassero (16-9).

The Mariners' first opponent would be the Baltimore Orioles. Although Seattle played the first two games in front of their home fans, the Orioles won both contests by identical 9-3 scores. Then the best-of-five series went to Baltimore, where Mariners avoided a sweep with a 4-2 win. In the fourth game, Randy Johnson struck out 13 batters and allowed just three runs, but Baltimore's Mike Mussina gave up just two hits. That was good enough for a 3-1 Orioles win that eliminated Seattle from the playoffs.

Alex had hit well, batting .313 for the series, but he was disappointed in the result. It had been a good year for the Mariners. The off-season, though, turned ugly as the solid Seattle team began to fracture. Star pitcher Randy Johnson was unhappy in Seattle and demanded a trade. And some friction began to appear between the team's two biggest stars, Ken Griffey and Alex Rodriguez. Griffey, the team's leader since he blossomed as a star in 1989, felt threatened by Rodriguez's own emergence, some observers felt.

"Other guys can have their share of the spotlight. It's not important to me," Griffey told *Sport* in an October 1997 article. "But when they get more than their share, then they say about me, 'You're not the star of the team.' But I'm the guy who has to take the responsibility. . . . I take the blame, but I never get the credit."

"It's accurate in a way," Alex responded. "That's why some people call him the best player in the game. That's why he makes $11, $12 million. I think it comes with the territory. . . . I don't think anyone receives more attention than him in the whole big leagues.

"I got a lot of attention last year, but I deserved it. And he's having a lot of attention this year. Great attention."

Alex had been stung by Griffey's comments, and he was hurt by the Mariners' quick playoff exit. Remembering how overwhelming the 1996 off-season had been, he decided to focus his attention on baseball during the winter months. "I said no to almost everything I was asked to do, unless it was charity stuff."

Alex did find time to work on an autobiography for children titled *Alex Rodriguez: Hit a Grand Slam* (1998, Taylor Publishing). He collaborated on the book with a Washington sportswriter named Greg Brown. *Hit a Grand Slam* is illustrated both with colored drawings and Alex's personal photographs, and in it Alex tells about his childhood, his baseball accomplishments, and his feelings about fame and money. "It's not how much you make that counts," he wrote. "It's what you do with it."

Alex took a step toward his own education by enrolling in his first college course. "I'm determined to get a college degree some day," he wrote in *Hit a Grand Slam*. "I don't care if it takes me 10 years."

He also went back to the Boys and Girls Club of Miami to hold his workouts with Eddy Rodriguez and the young players, and to attend the dedication of the new baseball field that he had helped to fund. The new playing facility was named the Alex Rodriguez Baseball Field in honor of his generosity.

"I'm really proud of that," Alex said. "It was dedicated January 24. It's got a bronze statue of me out front and my picture on a wall."

CHAPTER EIGHT
Perennial All-Star

Nineteen ninety-eight did not start out too well for Alex. In January, burglars broke into his house and stole nearly $100,000 worth of cash and personal items. Alex was so upset that he decided to sell his house. "I just picture in my mind these people going through my things, over and over. It's a disgusting feeling," Alex told the *Seattle Times*. "I'll never forget it. Miami is my home and people know me, and I had hoped they respected me to leave my stuff alone. Then this.... I want to leave, but it's my home, my hometown, you know? I don't know what to do." Alex moved into an apartment in Seattle and listed his house for sale.

He didn't let this off-the-field problem distract him from what he wanted to do on the baseball diamond. Alex's 1997 season had been good, but he wanted to put up MVP-type numbers again, as he had in 1996.

He seemed well on his way to doing just that. In three games April 18–20, Alex tied a 71-year-old American League record with eight extra-base hits—four doubles, two triples, and two home runs. On May 16, he had a two-homer, four-RBI game against Toronto, and he followed that by hitting safely in his next 12 games. On May 20, in the midst of this streak, Alex again hit two round-trippers—the sixth multi-homer game of his career and the third of the season.

Alex matched his 13-game hitting streak in May with another in June; he batted .328 for the month and

A group of young players watch entranced as Alex Rodriguez breaks down the elements of his swing at a baseball clinic.

was once again selected the American League's starting shortstop for the All-Star Game.

The 1998 contest was his best All-Star appearance to date. Before the game, he was invited to participate in the annual Home Run Derby; during the game he was 2-for-3 with a homer as the American League team won, 13-8.

Alex continued to pound the ball out of stadiums. He homered in three straight games in mid-July, hitting his 30th of the season on July 19. Two weeks later, on July 31, he stole his 29th and 30th bases of the year in a game against the Yankees. He was immediately congratulated by his friend Derek Jeter. The stolen bases had made Alex a member of the 30-30 Club, an exclusive group of players with the combination of power and speed to hit 30 homers and steal 30 bases. But although fewer than two dozen players were members of the 30-30 club, Alex had his eyes set on higher goals.

Alex racked up another long hitting streak in July and August, hitting in 12 straight games from July 30 to August 12. In the final game of that streak, he hit his 36th homer of the season, tying the career-high total he had set in 1996. Alex's hot hitting continued through August; he was 5-for-5 on August 18 in a game against Detroit, and he batted .347 for the month.

However, despite Alex's heroics and another great year by Ken Griffey, the Mariners were struggling. Randy Johnson had managed just a 9-10 record, and he was traded at the end of July to the Houston Astros for four minor-league prospects. Even though Seattle was leading the league in home runs, the team was in last place in the AL West at the end of August with a 61-71 record. There would be no playoffs at the end of this season for Alex Rodriguez.

Nonetheless, Alex continued to play hard. On September 8 he hit his 39th home run of the year, and on September 10 he went 2-for-4 and stole his 41st base of the season. But he seemed to be pressing after that, seeking his 40th homer of the year. Although he continued hitting—his average for the season remained around .307—Alex did not hit one out of the park for the next two weeks. Finally, on September 19, Alex connected on a first-inning Jack McDowell fastball and sent it over the wall in Anaheim to reach the milestone.

He went 3 for 4 in that game and reached another milestone with his 200th hit of the year.

Three days later, Alex blasted home run number 41 against Oakland, breaking the American League record for homers by a shortstop. The old mark, 40, had been set by Rico Petrocelli in 1969. He would finish with 42, establishing a new mark for AL shortstops.

Personally, 1998 was a great season for Alex. He played in every game, batting .310 and leading the league in hits (213), at bats (686), and multi-hit games (64). He was third in runs scored (123) and total bases (384). His 124 RBIs were the fifth-highest total in the league; his home run total was seventh best; and he swiped 46 bases.

As Alex watches, these elementary school–age players take part in a fielding drill. Alex enjoys putting on baseball clinics for young players in the off-season.

Alex demonstrates the fundamentals to admiring young fans.

Despite these great numbers, as well as Griffey's second straight year with 56 home runs, the 1998 Mariners managed just a third-place finish in the AL West with a 76-85 record.

In the off-season, Alex responded to fan messages. During the year, he and his brother Joe had put together an Internet Web page, Arod.com, that gave updates on Alex's progress, included a regular diary of his thoughts, and invited fans to submit questions via e-mail for Alex to answer. The response was overwhelming.

Alex continued his charity work, as well as the Grand Slam for Kids program in Seattle schools, and he spent time with his girlfriend, Cynthia Scurtis, a

Miami resident whom he had been dating for about a year.

The questions about Alex Rodriguez and Ken Griffey's futures with the Mariners continued to swirl. A new ballpark was being built for the team in Seattle, but the cost was tremendous—nearly $400 million. A-rod and Junior could both be free agents after the 2000 season, and some experts believed that they could each command long-term contracts totalling $200 million. Would Seattle, a small-market team, be able to hold on to both of its superstar players?

The questions and rumors would continue to swirl as the 1999 season began. Alex made no secret of his preference to play for a team that had a chance to

At his clinic, Alex talks to the rapt audience about the importance of working hard in school.

win the World Series. On his Web site, he wrote, "I talked with management during spring training about their plans for me. I asked if they would try to trade me this season, and they said no. . . . But the bottom line is what direction this team wants to go. Does management want to hang around in the middle of the pack or make the moves necessary to win a championship?"

Alex's 1999 season was disrupted by more than just the question of where he would play in a few years. In the second game of the season, he injured his knee and took himself out of the game. The knee would require surgery, and he missed the team's next 32 games.

Without their star shortstop, the Mariners played poorly. The team was just 15-20 before Alex returned to the lineup in a game against the Kansas City Royals on May 21. Alex homered in his first at-bat and went 2 for 4 with a stolen base, but the Royals won the game 12-7. Alex went hitless in the next game, an 11-10 Kansas City victory that dropped the Mariners seven games below .500.

Then A-rod led Seattle to a six-game winning streak in which he hit .304 with three homers. The Mariners dropped the next two games, then ripped off four straight wins to pull their record back over .500 at 25-24. Over the next two weeks, Alex went on a 13-game hitting streak in which he raised his average to .357 and his home-run total to nine. In one contest during that span, a loss to Baltimore, he stole the 100th base of his career.

But Alex's average dropped back to .300 by the end of June, and it stayed at that level for the rest of the summer. The team leveled off as well.

After A-Rod hit his 34th and 35th home runs of the year in an 11-4 win over the Chicago White Sox on August 13, he went into the worst slump of his career. He batted just .104 over the next month, and his average fell from .315 to .287. Finally, on September 16, he seemed to break out of his funk with a grand-slam home run in the eighth inning that powered the Mariners to a 4-3 win over Tampa Bay.

Alex hit .268 the rest of the way and finished with the lowest batting average of his major-league career, .285. However, he did drive in 111 runs and tied his own mark with 42 homers, even though he played in just 129 games. And despite the knee injury, he still stole 21 bases and hit 25 doubles.

For the Mariners and their fans, it was another disappointing season. The team finished third in the American League West again, this time with a 79-83 record. A highlight was the completion of SAFECO Field, the team's new baseball-only stadium. The Mariners played their first game at the new park on July 15 and went 23-19 in their new home during the second half.

As the season drew to a close, Alex repeated his desire to remain with Seattle—but only with the right contract, and only if the Mariners would make the off-season moves needed to be playoff contenders again. He warned the team that if they traded him because the management was afraid they would lose him to free agency after the 2000 season, he would not sign a contract extension with his new team. This would make it difficult for Seattle to get equal value in return for their star, because the team that Alex was traded to might lose him to free agency at the end of the season.

Alex slides into third and glances at home. Going into the 2000 season, he was not sure which team would become his home after his contract expired.

"The only thing they can do is go out and make us a championship ballclub," he commented. "That's what I've said all along. If they go out and get the pieces, sure, I'd be more than willing to sign with the Mariners. I've always said that's where I want to be under the right conditions. And the right conditions are having a championship ballclub like Texas, the Yankees, and Cleveland."

In October, Mariners chairman Howard Lincoln told the media that the team had made lucrative offers to both Griffey and Rodriguez. The contracts would make them the highest-paid players in baseball, Lincoln said, and he hoped to sign Alex soon. But Rodriguez said he wasn't ready.

"I haven't even thought about baseball the last couple of weeks," he admitted. "I'm just focusing on working out, getting my knee ready for another big-league year. I'm not concerned about my contract or any of that stuff."

In the fall of 1999, Griffey, who was also dealing with the uncertainty of the situation, advised his younger teammate, "Hey, you've got 18 months. Don't say anything. Just go out and play. You're not going to make up your mind right now, because it's impossible."

The relationship between the two stars seemed to have matured. "We've never had a falling out," Griffey commented. "It's like a big brother–little brother relationship. I try to make sure he keeps right."

"I don't know how I [will] deal with [the contract situation]," Rodriguez admitted in a *Sporting News* interview. "I've never been under such a microscope. I guess the way you deal with it is to be honest with people. You speak from your heart. But I don't know. I'm not experienced with this. It's not like fielding a ground ball or hitting the curve. I guess [I'll] sit back and weigh all my options. It's another 18 months, and we'll see what's to be."

Whatever will happen in Alex's future, it is almost certain that the All-Star shortstop will leave a lasting mark on the game of baseball. After all, he will just be turning just 25 in the 2000 season, his fifth full year in the major leagues. The best years of his career should be ahead of him. There is every reason to expect that Alex Rodriguez will continue to improve over the next 10 years.

"He's already a complete player," Rudy Terrasas, a scout with the Texas Rangers, told the *Sporting News*. "He can beat you in all facets of the game—with his power, his speed, and his glove. And he's still young, with a tremendous upside. People who play like he does are usually 28, 29, 30 years old."

And whatever he accomplishes on the field, it's certain that his off-the-field accomplishments, such as his work with students, hospital visits, and charitable donations—as well as his status as a good-looking, single multimillionaire—will also continue to draw attention. "He's Mr. Clean," said teammate David Segui. "He's milk and cookies. He doesn't like to hear that, but he is. He likes everybody in here to think he's some kind of thug from Miami, but he's as milk-and-cookies as it gets. This heartthrob thing? It's for real. . . . But he's very respectful. He's a good guy." And girlfriend Cynthia Scurtis has said, "People fall in love with his image. . . . They love the idea of Alex. They love his smile. He's very attractive. . . . People are always telling me, 'Oh, he's 23, he so good-looking, he has all this money. How can you trust him?' But all you have to do [to trust him] is know him. That's all."

She also has an opinion on his views on superstardom. "Deep down in his heart, does he want to be the one they're always talking about? I honestly don't know. I think it would be inhuman not to want that. But he never expresses it. I just see how hard he works, and I wish sometimes that there was a little more recognition. But you know what? He's going to be around for a very long time. And in the end, the recognition will be there."

Alex Rodriguez himself once said, "I want to be known as a good major-leaguer, and good major-leaguers work to become good." There is not doubt that as long as A-Rod continues working, he is destined to be more than good—perhaps even to be the best shortstop of all time.

CHRONOLOGY

1975   Alexander Emmanuel Rodriguez born to Victor and Lourdes Navarro Rodriguez on July 27

1979   The Rodriguez family moves from New York City to the Dominican Republic

1983   The Rodriguez family returns to the United States, settling in a suburb of Miami, Florida

1984   Victor Rodriguez leaves his family for New York City

1990   Juan Diego Arteaga, who had acted as Alex's surrogate father, dies

1992   Leads Westminster Christian to both state and national baseball championships; selected as High School All-American; plays with the U.S. Junior National baseball team in Mexico; again named to the All-State football team as a quarterback

1993   Chosen first in the 1993 amateur baseball draft by the Seattle Mariners; begins pro career in the Arizona Instructional League

1994   Plays at all four major-league levels

1995   Joins the majors for the pennant race on August 31; participates in first-round playoff victory over the New York Yankees

1996   Has breakthrough season, leading the league in batting (.358), hits (215), runs (141), doubles (54), and total bases (379); finishes second, by three votes, in MVP balloting

1997   Hits for the cycle on June 5 against the Detroit Tigers

1998   Autobiography for children, *Alex Rodriguez: Hit a Grand Slam*, is published; baseball field is dedicated in his name at the Boys and Girls Club of Miami; sets new record for shortstops with 42 home runs and becomes just the third player in baseball history to record more than 40 homers and 40 steals; with brother Joe, establishes Web site Arod.com

1999   Misses 32 games because of knee injury early in the season; matches career high with 42 home runs

MAJOR-LEAGUE STATS

Year	Team	G	AB	R	H	2B	3B	HR	RBI	BB	AVG
1994	Sea	17	54	4	11	0	0	0	2	3	.204
1995	Sea	48	142	15	33	6	2	5	19	6	.232
1996	Sea	146	601	141	215	54	1	36	123	59	.358
1997	Sea	141	587	100	176	40	3	23	84	41	300
1998	Sea	161	686	123	213	35	5	42	124	45	.310
1999	Sea	129	502	110	143	25	0	42	111	56	.285
Totals		642	2572	493	791	160	11	148	463	210	.280

INDEX